Cinderella

FAY'S FAIRY TALES

Cinderella

William Wegman

WITH CAROLE KISMARIC AND MARVIN HEIFERMAN

HYPERION
NEW YORK

NCE UPON A TIME there lived a rich widowed gentlemen and his lovely young daughter. Ella, as she was named, was beautiful and intelligent. She caused her father no trouble at all, but he thought she needed a mother's attention. He married a woman who had two daughters about Ella's age. This seemed like a perfect arrangement, but before he could find out otherwise, he died.

Ella quickly learned that a smiling stepmother was not necessarily a good sign. She smiled with each new chore and thankless task she thought up for Ella—like beating rugs and scrubbing the kitchen floor. She smiled when she pointed to the attic and said to Ella, "Go to your room. From now on this is where you will sleep."

One of Ella's many chores was sweeping and cleaning the chimneys, fireplaces, and cellar. It was a particularly dirty job but one that Ella carried out cheerfully, for it was not in Ella's nature to complain, nor was she offended by the nicknames inflicted upon her. "Ashcan Ella," said the eldest stepsister. "Cellarella," trumpeted the younger. "Cinderella!" they chimed in unison. And the name stuck.

One day a letter came by messenger.

BY INVITATION

of

THE KING

COME ONE AND ALL
TO A GALA BALL

AT THE GRAND PALACE
THE FIRST DAY OF NEXT WEEK

Everyone knew that the real reason for the ball was to find a bride for the king's son, the very handsome, very eligible young prince.

The stepmother was agitated beyond belief. "Only a few days to prepare," she complained. There was no question in her mind that the prince would choose one of her own daughters to be his wife. Of that she was certain. The only question was, which one?

The stepsisters were in a tizzy. "Cinders, sweet thing, would you please add an appliqué to my dress?" "Ella, could you please hem my blue dress just in case I want to wear it?"

 Cinderella had hopes of going to the ball, too, but they were dashed by her stepmother. It seemed her ball gown had been sent overseas by mistake. At least that was what the stepmother claimed.

 LL DAY and into the next, Cinderella helped her sisters dress and redress. At last the carriage came to take the sisters to the ball. As she watched the coach disappear over the horizon, Cinderella thought: What if I make my own dress? Then I could go to the ball! Determined to try, she went off to the workroom. There she found some leftover scraps and managed to piece together a gown. Looking down at her tattered sandals, however, Cinderella realized that without proper shoes she could never go to the ball. Defeated, Cinderella slowly climbed the long staircase to her room, where she cried herself to sleep.

She awakened to a glowing light. Turning toward the window, she saw before her a vision so lovely, radiant, and serene it could only be...

"Cinderella, I am your Fairy Godmother," a sweet voice said. The beautiful fairy waved her magic wand, drawing Cinderella to her. Together they floated down into the garden.

"I am here to grant your wish. I understand you want to go to the ball. First you need a carriage. Go get me a pumpkin. Over there, that nice big fat one." *Zap!* All at once, the pumpkin was transformed into a beautiful golden carriage.

"Now you will need a debonair footman. Fetch me that charming rat in the basement." Obediently Cinderella returned with the creature and placed it on the ground before the Fairy Godmother, who, with a flick of her wand, transformed the rat into a debonair footman.

"And now, for a fine coachman to drive your coach. Over there…," she said, pointing, "this lizard will do perfectly. Place it upon your fair head."

"Really?" said Cinderella, but she obeyed. *Zap!* The splendid green coachman seemed as amazed by the transformation as was Cinderella.

"And how about those little garden mice?" the Fairy Godmother continued. Cinderella ran to the garden and returned with two handfuls, six mice to be exact. And with six taps of the Fairy Godmother's magic wand they became the most noble, spirited coach horses in all the land.

"Now you are ready for the ball. Except…"

"Except for the way I'm dressed!"

"No problem. Voilà." Then the Fairy Godmother pointed the magic wand at Cinderella and turned Cinderella's frock into the most beautiful gown in the world, complete with matching corsage and tiara. Cinderella's sandals became the most beautiful glass slippers that ever were.

"Look, they glow!" exclaimed Cinderella.

"Now you are ready to go to the ball, Cinderella, but you must be home by midnight," the Fairy Godmother warned her. "At the stroke of twelve, all becomes as it once was—the coach will turn back into a pumpkin, your footman will once again be a rat, the coachman a lizard, the six fine horses six mice, and your beautiful gown nothing more than your tattered frock."

"I promise," said Cinderella.

At the castle, the ball was in full swing. But the prince was not exactly having the time of his life. Frankly, he was a bit bored, particularly by two sisters who stuck to him like frosting on a cake.

UDDENLY a mysterious guest arrived. For a moment the orchestra stopped playing. A hush swept the room.

"I must know who she is," said the prince. The mysterious guest was so beautiful that the prince found himself unable to talk. But shyness soon eased, and before long they were dancing. First a gavotte, then a minuet, then the daring waltz. Where did she learn to dance this way? It was as if she were transported by her special glass slippers. Not even her own stepsisters could guess that this was Cinderella. They were beside themselves with jealousy.

Cinderella was so happy—her feet never quite seemed to touch the ground as she danced and danced. Suddenly she remembered the words of her Fairy Godmother. She rushed to the window. "Oh no!" exclaimed Cinderella. The clock in the castle court-yard read 11:59. Inside, the great gilded clock began to strike twelve: *Bong! Bong! Bong!* Cinderella fled in a panic. Across the crowded ballroom floor and through the castle halls she ran. At the top of the stair-case, she tripped, leaving behind one glass slipper.

It was too late to turn back. She descended the grand staircase and fled the castle, racing past a lizard, six brown mice, a rat, and a sad-looking pumpkin. She ran and ran into the night, her once fine gown disintegrating behind her.

At last she reached home, dressed in her humble paisley frock, still holding one glass slipper. She hid the slipper in the basement, where no one would find it.

What an evening! She had only spent a few hours with the prince, yet she would never forget him.

Her reverie was broken by the unmistakable chatter of her stepsisters. They could hardly wait to tell Cinderella all about their extraordinary evening, and especially how the prince was so smitten, first with one, then the other. No mention was made of the mysterious "princess."

EANWHILE, the prince was in a state of great distress. His dog, Robaire, led the prince to the head of the grand stairway, where he had found the lost glass slipper. The sight of the tiny delicate shoe made his heart ache. Who was she? How would he ever find her? All he had was her glass slipper. He made a vow to search every household in the kingdom for her. He would dispatch his own royal emissary and the maiden whose foot fit perfectly into the slipper would be his princess.

Day after day the shoe bearer went from house to house in search of the maiden, but to no avail.

When the royal shoe bearer arrived at her house, Cinderella was busy sweeping the basement. The stepsisters practically trampled the poor fellow in their efforts to be the first to try on the coveted slipper. Both of the sisters' feet looked huge next to the delicate slipper.

As the shoe bearer was leaving, he heard a noise in the basement. "Who's there?" he asked. "Only Cinderella," chimed the stepsisters. "And we know that she did not go to the ball!"

"Nevertheless," said the shoe bearer, "I am under oath to the prince that no fair foot be left untried. Present her!" he demanded.

The emissary went down the dark stairs to the basement. Cinderella stopped sweeping. She came forward and effortlessly slid her foot into the slipper.

The stepsisters were shocked. "What an impossible coincidence!" said the eldest. "Yes, a freak occurrence!" said the youngest. All doubt vanished, however, when Cinderella produced the slipper's mate.

The shoe bearer said urgently, "Cinderella, we must go immediately to the castle."

ACK AT THE CASTLE, the prince paced and fretted on the balcony. When he caught sight of the royal carriage, he knew that the princess had been found at last. He raced through the castle and into the courtyard, arriving just in time to help Cinderella from the carriage. They gazed into each other's eyes and knew that they were in love.

Soon they were married. And what a spectacular wedding it was! Everyone was invited, even Cinderella's stepmother and her two stepsisters, who, after the wedding, moved into the castle where Cinderella and the prince lived happily ever after.

Text and photographs copyright ©1993 by William Wegman.
Printed in Hong Kong by South China Printing Company Ltd.
Design: Empire Design Studio
For information address Hyperion Books for Children,
114 Fifth Avenue, New York, New York 10011-5690.
First Mini Edition 1999
1 3 5 7 9 10 8 6 4 2
Library of Congress Cataloging-in-Publication Data
Wegman, William.
Cinderella / William Wegman, with Carole Kismaric
and Marvin Keiferman—1st ed.
p. cm. – (Fay's fairy tales)
Summary: In her haste to flee the palace before her fairy godmother's
magic loses effect, Cinderella leaves behind a glass slipper.
Photographs show the characters depicted as dogs.
ISBN 0-7868-0550-1 (mini edition)
[1. Fairy tales.] I. Kismaric, Carole. II. Keiferman, Marvin. III. Title.
IV. Series: Wegman, William. Fay's fairy tales.
PZ8.W424Ci 1993
398.21—dc20
[E] 92-72028

ACKNOWLEDGMENTS
With thanks to
Virginia Alexander, Andrea Beeman, Alison Berry, Nancy Boas, Judith Bobb,
Jason Burch, Christine Burgin, Lely Constantinople, David Corey,
Suzanne Farrell, Stacy Fischer, Lance Fung, Pamela Gaul, Sharon and Gregg
Hartmann, Susanne Lipshutz, Susan Litecky, Pat and Connie O'Brien,
John Reuter, Lynda Rodolitz, Dale Rubin, Steve Rubin, Robert Vissichio,
Jeanette Ward, Pam Wegman, W.J. Fantasy, and The Pace/MacGill Gallery.

Cinderella was developed and edited by William Wegman with
Marvin Keiferman and Carole Kismaric/Lookout Books, New York.